'H' Patten was brought up in Birmingham in a close-knit Jamaican community. His many talents include choreography and dance, storytelling, illustration and documentary film-making. A founder member of Dance de L'Afrique, he has performed and choreographed in leading dance companies in Britain, Africa and the Caribbean. He has worked with children and young adults in Soweto, ,South Africa, and with young offenders in Britain. This is his first book.

John Clementson is both a freelance illustrator and Senior Lecturer in Illustration at the University of Wolverhampton. He has created four board books for very young children, and has illustrated three of Michael Rosen's picture books: *How the Animals Got Their Colours, The First Giraffe* and *Crow and Hawk* (all Studio Editions). This is his first book for Frances Lincoln.

To my children, Mawuena, Kwesi, Onayomi and Omoyele,
and all my family, friends and fore-parents who have passed
the stories down over the generations, inspiring this new tale. – 'H'

For Alan, Billy, Dorothy and Little R. – J.C.

First published in Great Britain in 1999 by
Frances Lincoln Children's Books, 4 Torriano Mews,
Torriano Avenue, London NW5 2RZ
www.franceslincoln.com

First paperback edition 2000

British Library Cataloguing in Publication Data available on request

ISBN 978-0-7112-1401-9

Set in Hiroshige Medium

Printed in China

5 7 9 8 6

Clever Anansi and Boastful Bullfrog

A Caribbean Tale

'H' Patten

Illustrated by
John Clementson

F

FRANCES LINCOLN
CHILDREN'S BOOKS

Once upon a time, not all bullfrogs
were plain like their cousins, the lizards.
Bredda Croaky was a special bullfrog.
His skin glowed with all the rich colours
of hibiscus flowers. He used to croak
all day long, so that the other animals
would admire him.

Anansi the spider didn't like this. He grew jealous of Bredda Croaky and tired of his boastful croaking.

One day, he decided to put a stop to it. He sat down and thought hard. Suddenly he had an idea: "If Bredda Croaky had an enemy, 'im would have to hide from them, and 'im couldn't croak out loud no more."

Anansi set out to find Bredda Croaky an enemy!

He went down to the big mango tree at the crossroads,
hoping to catch Bredda Puss on his way home from the market.

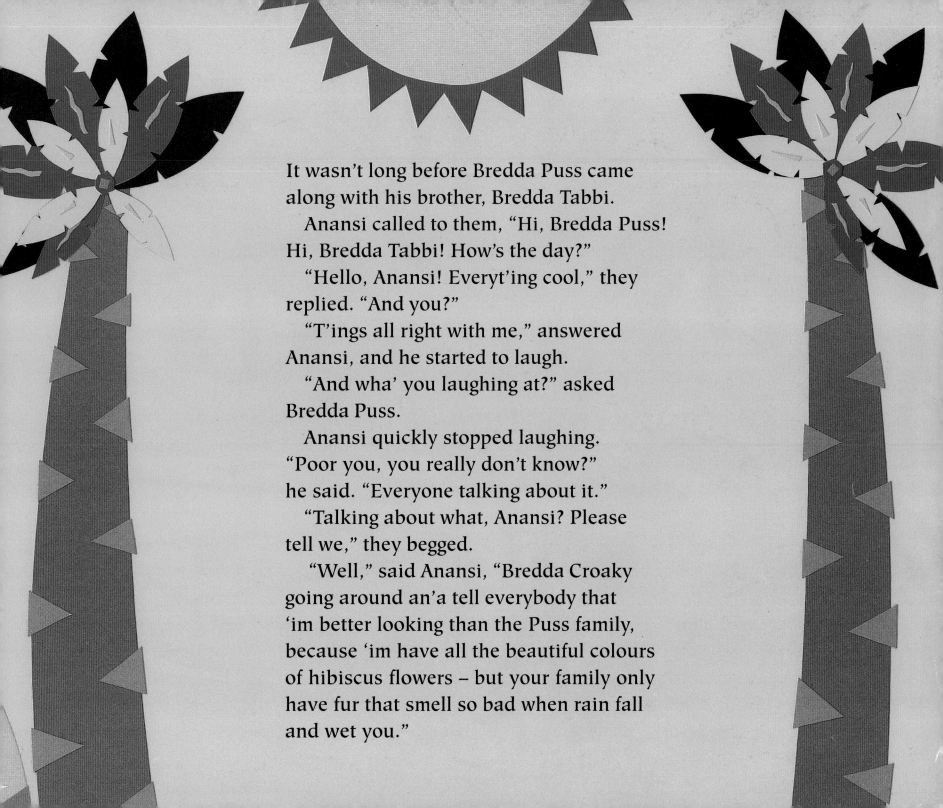

It wasn't long before Bredda Puss came along with his brother, Bredda Tabbi.

Anansi called to them, "Hi, Bredda Puss! Hi, Bredda Tabbi! How's the day?"

"Hello, Anansi! Everyt'ing cool," they replied. "And you?"

"T'ings all right with me," answered Anansi, and he started to laugh.

"And wha' you laughing at?" asked Bredda Puss.

Anansi quickly stopped laughing. "Poor you, you really don't know?" he said. "Everyone talking about it."

"Talking about what, Anansi? Please tell we," they begged.

"Well," said Anansi, "Bredda Croaky going around an'a tell everybody that 'im better looking than the Puss family, because 'im have all the beautiful colours of hibiscus flowers – but your family only have fur that smell so bad when rain fall and wet you."

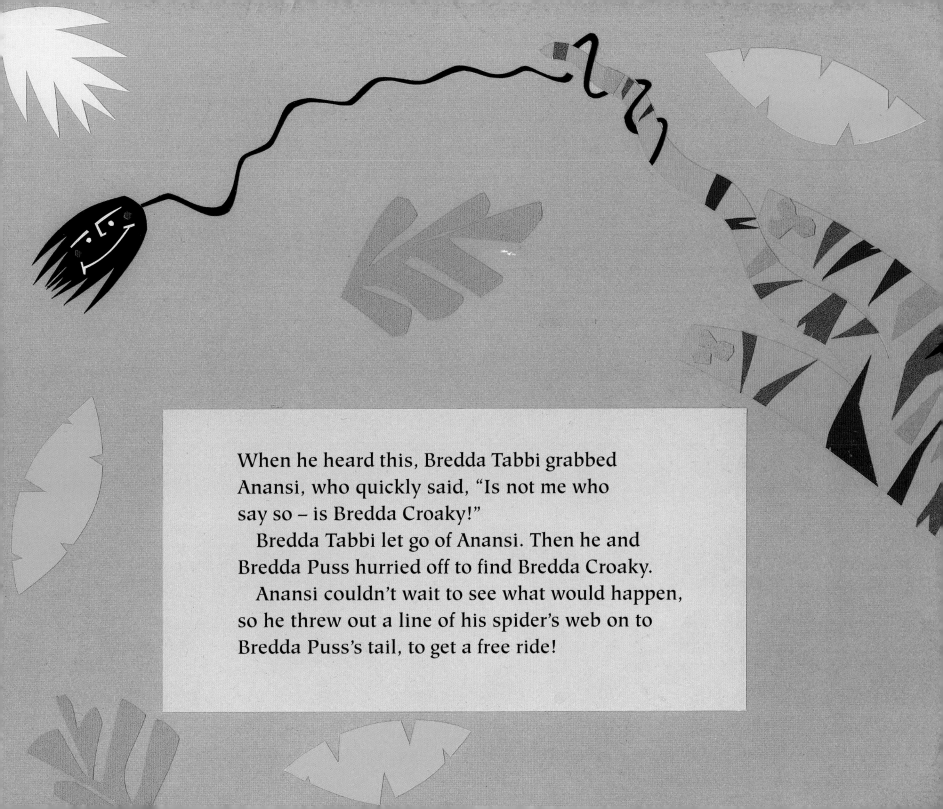

When he heard this, Bredda Tabbi grabbed
Anansi, who quickly said, "Is not me who
say so – is Bredda Croaky!"

Bredda Tabbi let go of Anansi. Then he and
Bredda Puss hurried off to find Bredda Croaky.

Anansi couldn't wait to see what would happen,
so he threw out a line of his spider's web on to
Bredda Puss's tail, to get a free ride!

They soon found Bredda Croaky down by the river.
He was croaking loudly and, as usual, showing off
his beautiful skin. In fact, he was so busy showing
off to the other animals that he didn't see Bredda Puss
and Bredda Tabbi coming.

They pushed their way through the
admiring crowd. Bredda Tabbi grabbed
Bredda Croaky by the neck, while
Bredda Puss grabbed Bredda Croaky's
feet and the tiny piece of tail left from
Bredda Croaky's younger days as a tadpole.
They both began to pull.

Bredda Croaky's body started to stretch.
The colour began to drain from him,
and his tail grew longer and longer.

Poor Bredda Croaky struggled and croaked loudly in protest, but they would not let go.

All this noise woke
Bredda Patoo Owl
from an afternoon
sleep in his tree.
Grumbling to himself,
he flew down to find
out what was happening.
  When he saw Bredda
Puss and Bredda Tabbi
fighting over Bredda
Croaky, he hooted,
"STOP!"

Bredda Puss and Bredda Tabbi dropped
Bredda Croaky, and the animals froze –
for they all respected wise old Bredda Patoo.

"What's going on?" asked Bredda Patoo.
"You woke me from a wonderful dream."

Bredda Tabbi cried, "Anansi tell we how
Bredda Croaky have everyone laughing
and talking about how 'im better looking
than me and Bredda Puss."

"Yes, and 'im say that we only have fur,"
said Bredda Puss.

"… that smell so bad when rain catch us,"
added Bredda Tabbi.

Bredda Croaky couldn't believe his ears.
"Is *lie* Anansi telling," he said.

"Is the first time we hearing this!" said
the other animals. "Is really *lie* Anansi telling."

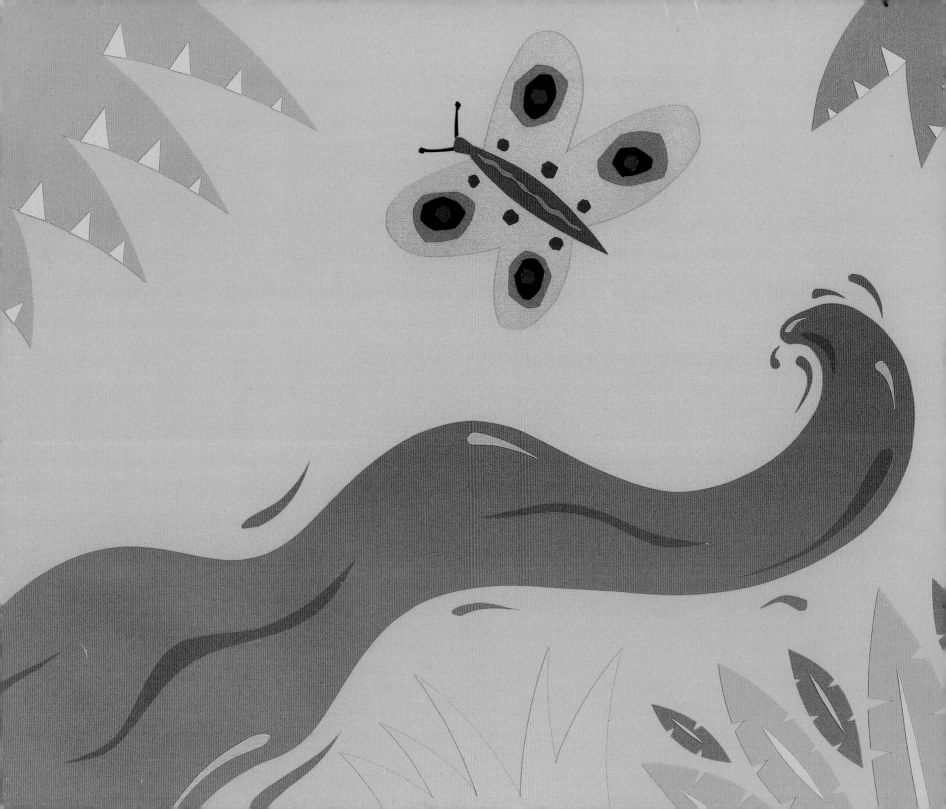

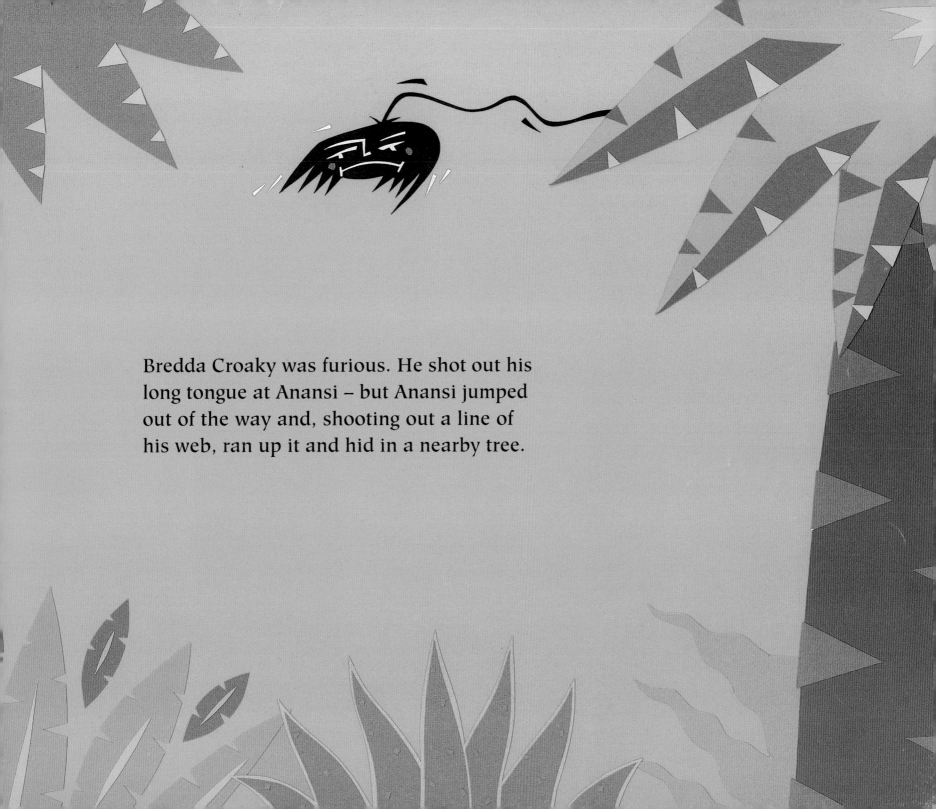

Bredda Croaky was furious. He shot out his
long tongue at Anansi – but Anansi jumped
out of the way and, shooting out a line of
his web, ran up it and hid in a nearby tree.

Bredda Puss and Bredda Tabbi turned to
Bredda Croaky to apologise – but what
they saw made them burst out laughing.
All the other animals looked, and began
laughing too.

"What you all laughing at?" asked
Bredda Croaky crossly, but none of
the animals could bring themselves
to tell him.

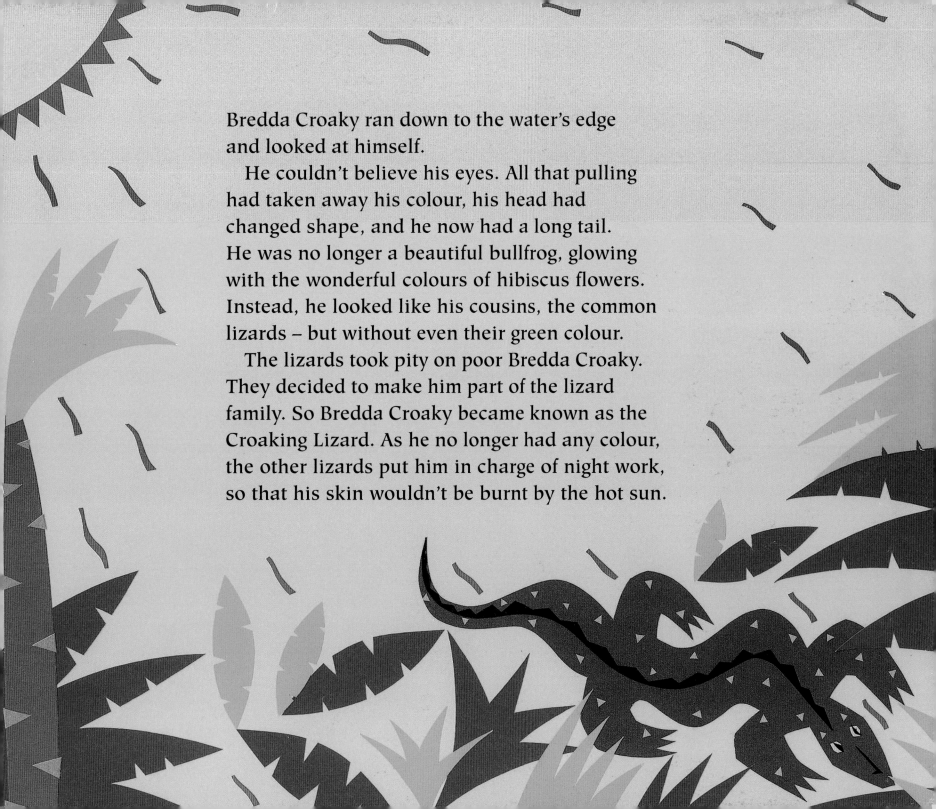

Bredda Croaky ran down to the water's edge
and looked at himself.

He couldn't believe his eyes. All that pulling
had taken away his colour, his head had
changed shape, and he now had a long tail.
He was no longer a beautiful bullfrog, glowing
with the wonderful colours of hibiscus flowers.
Instead, he looked like his cousins, the common
lizards – but without even their green colour.

The lizards took pity on poor Bredda Croaky.
They decided to make him part of the lizard
family. So Bredda Croaky became known as the
Croaking Lizard. As he no longer had any colour,
the other lizards put him in charge of night work,
so that his skin wouldn't be burnt by the hot sun.

From that day to this, Bredda Croaky
took to croaking after dark. His croaking
joined the chirping of Bredda Cricky,
the cricket, and became known all over
the world as part of the tropical night song.
Is Anansi mek it so.

Jack mandora mi nuh choose none.

Although I am the one who has told
you this story, if others say it's not true,
don't come back to me about it.

Anansi Stories

Anansi is a special, magical character. Sometimes he is a spider, sometimes a man and sometimes a little bit of both. In Africa and the Caribbean, Anansi is considered a teacher, one of the first teachers most children have. When Anansi does wrong, he teaches the consequences of doing bad things. When he does good, he also teaches the rewards of doing good.

Anansi stories came originally from the Ashanti region of Ghana, West Africa, and travelled to the Caribbean along with many thousands of African people. There more Anansi stories were created, thrilling generations of Caribbean children. Along with the African storytelling traditions, some of these later tales brought wild animals from Africa into a new setting.

When telling an Anansi story in the Caribbean, it is usual for the speaker to finish by saying, 'Jack mandora mi nuh choose none.' This line acknowledges that the stories may explain how different things came to exist in the world, but they are not meant to be factually correct, so '...if others say it's not true, don't come back to me about it'.

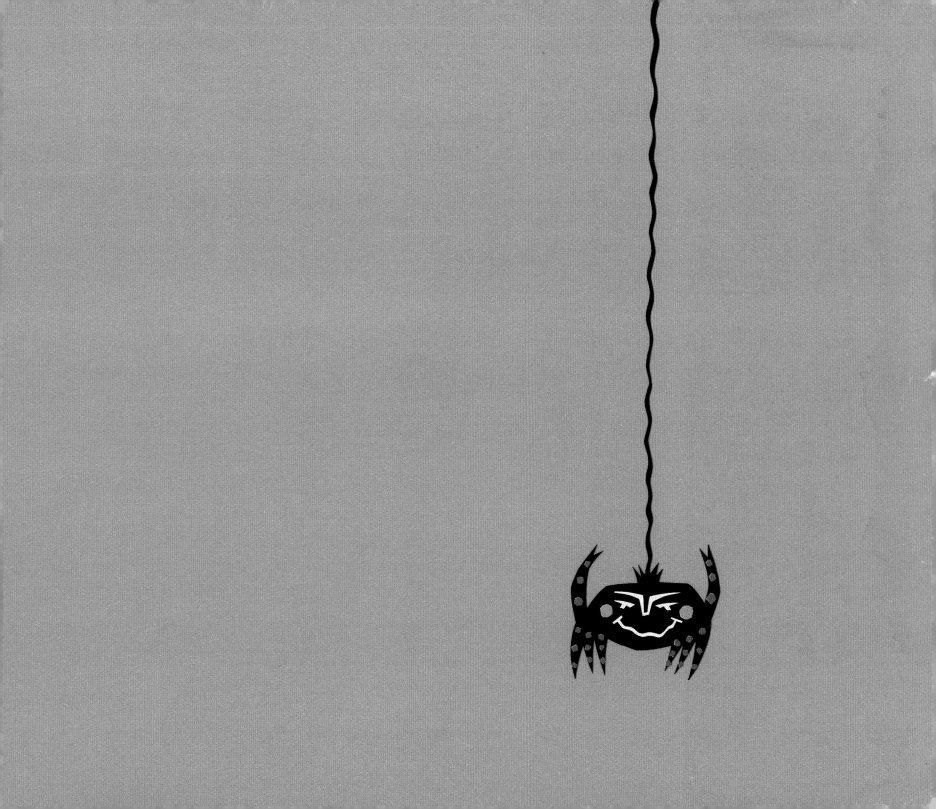

MORE TITLES FROM
FRANCES LINCOLN CHILDREN'S BOOKS

The Fire Children

Eric Maddern

Illustrated by Frané Lessac

Why are some people black, some white and others pink or brown?
This intriguing West African creation myth tells how the first spirit
people solve their loneliness using clay and fire – and fill the
Earth with children of every colour under the sun!

ISBN 978-184507-514-9

Rainbow Bird

Eric Maddern

Illustrated by Adrienne Kennaway

"I'm boss for fire," growls rough, tough Crocodile Man,
and he keeps the rest of the world cold and dark, until one day
clever Bird Woman sees her opportunity and seizes it…
An Aboriginal fire myth, lit with glowing illustrations.

ISBN 978-0-7112-0898-8

Anancy and Mr Dry-Bone

Fiona French

Penniless Anancy and rich Mr Dry-Bone both want to marry
Miss Louise, but she wants to marry the man who can make her laugh.
An original story, based on characters from traditional
Caribbean and West African folk tales.

ISBN 978-0-7112-0787-5

Frances Lincoln titles are available from all good bookshops.
You can also buy books and find out more about your favourite titles,
authors and illustrators on our website: www.franceslincoln.com